T0194900

If I Could Create a Tree Today

How Old Will It Be Tomorrow?

WRITTEN BY GLEN NAVIS

ILLUSTRATED BY TANYA PANOVA

Interior Art Credit: Tanya Panova

WestBow Press books may be ordered through booksellers or by contacting:

WestBow Press
A Division of Thomas Nelson & Zondervan
1663 Liberty Drive
Bloomington, IN 47403
www.westbowpress.com
1 (866) 928-1240

Because of the dynamic nature of the Internet, any web addresses or links contained in this book may have changed since publication and may no longer be valid. The views expressed in this work are solely those of the author and do not necessarily reflect the views of the publisher, and the publisher hereby disclaims any responsibility for them.

Any people depicted in stock imagery provided by Getty Images are models, and such images are being used for illustrative purposes only.
Certain stock imagery © Getty Images.

ISBN: 978-1-9736-2894-1 (sc)
ISBN: 978-1-9736-2895-8 (e)

Library of Congress Control Number: 2018906000

Print information available on the last page.

WestBow Press rev. date: 06/05/2019

WESTBOW
PRESS®
A DIVISION OF THOMAS NELSON
& ZONDERVAN

If I Could Create a Tree Today

How Old Will It Be Tomorrow?

I had a chance the other day
to hear once again
The age of this old mighty earth
proclaimed by learned men

"Six billion Four hundred million years"
stated as a fact
Made me wonder why they sound so sure –
the humility they lack

They said "We count the rings of trees

The depth of mountain canyons,

And layers of river stone.

The height of cinder cone."

Then I mused, what does this prove?
Does Creation not belong?
Has science proved beyond a doubt
the Bible must be wrong?

But what if for, just one prayer,

I had God's power to create

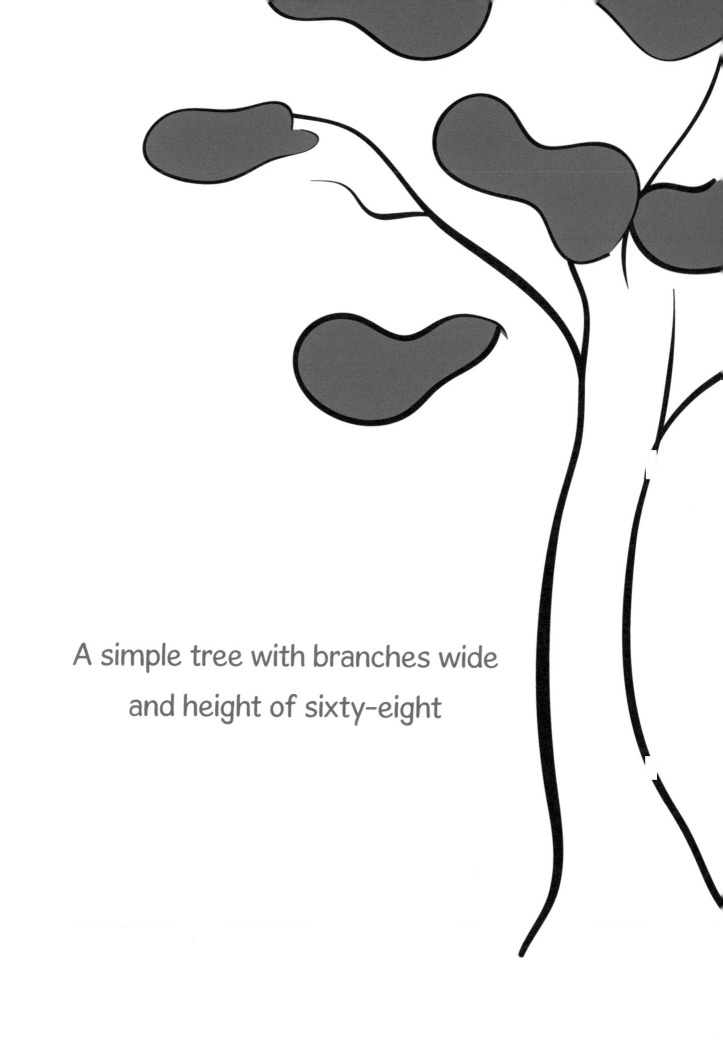

A simple tree with branches wide
and height of sixty-eight

And, next day, a scientist, on a
quest its age to know

Cut down the tree to count the
rings – just what would that show?

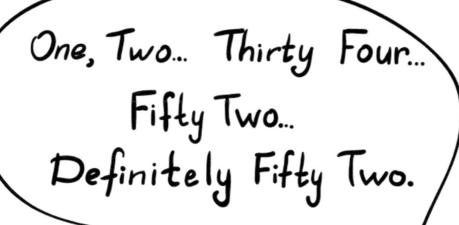

Would he declare "the tree is one day old"

as I, its creator knew

Or count the rings and state beyond a doubt

"the tree is fifty-two"

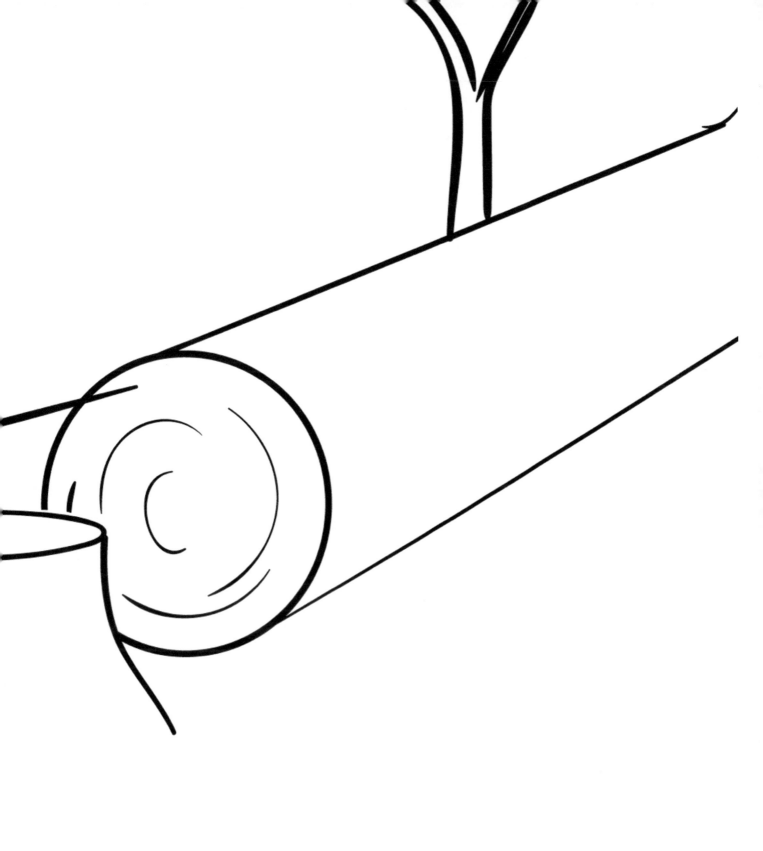

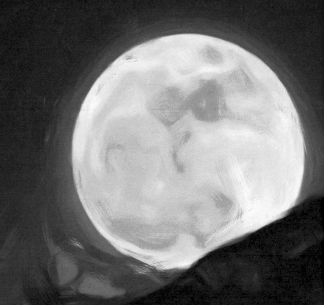

And what if, to carry on this thought,
when God Creation designed
Had created the sky looking
just one day old

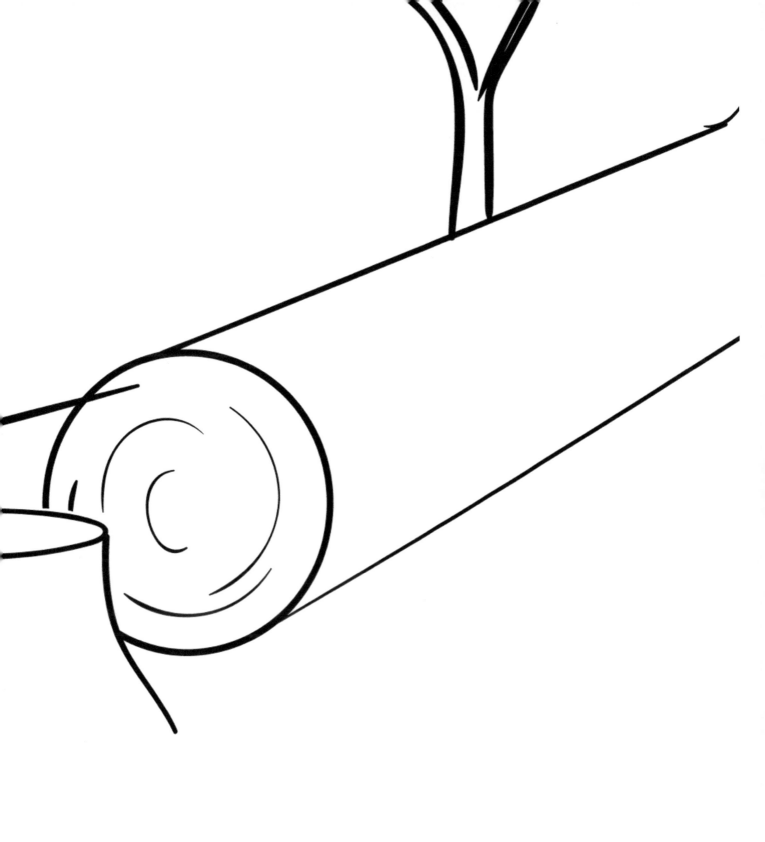

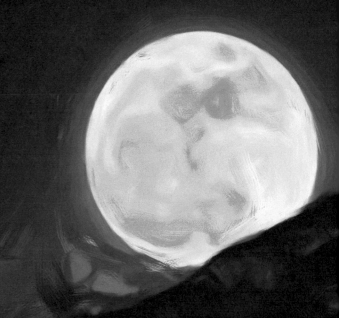

And what if, to carry on this thought,

when God Creation designed

Had created the sky looking

just one day old

Would we ever call it

Grand,

Amazing,

Incredibly Awesome,

Sublime!

Inspired by my brother, Arlyn Navis,
and Ark-Encounter

If I Could Create a Tree Today
(How Old Will it Be Tomorrow?)
GLEN NAVIS

I had a chance the other day to hear once again

The age of this old mighty earth proclaimed by learned men

"Six billion, four hundred million years" stated as a fact

Made me wonder why they sound so sure - the humility they lack

They said "we count the rings of trees and layers of river stone

The depth of mountain canyons, the height of cinder cone."

Then I mused, what does this prove? Does Creation not belong?

Has science proved beyond a doubt the Bible must be wrong?

But, what if for, just one prayer, I had God's power to create

A simple tree with branches wide and height of sixty-eight

And, next day, a scientist, on a quest its age to know

Cut down the tree to count the rings - just what would that show?

Would he declare "the tree is one day old" - as I, its creator, - knew

Or count the rings and state beyond a doubt - "the tree is fifty-two."

And what if, to carry on this thought, when God Creation designed

Had created a sky looking just one day old, would we ever call it

Grand, Amazing, Incredibly Awesome, Sublime!

Glen Navis is a retired CPA turned musician. He lives in Wisconsin with his wife LaVerne and her dog Shirley.

Printed in the United States
By Bookmasters